DETROIT PUBLIC LIBRARY

3 5674 03729146 6

CHASE BRANCH LIBRARY
17731 W. SEVEN MILE RD.
DETROIT, MI 48235

FEB - 2004

For music, sunshine and my daughter,
who has both in her eyes   —OE

Illustrations © 2003 by Ora Eitan.
Words and music by Ella Fitzgerald and Van Alexander
© 1938 (renewed 1966) EMI Robbins Catalog Inc.
All rights controlled by EMI Robbins Catalog Inc.
(Publishing) and Warner Bros. Publications U.S. Inc. All
rights reserved. Used by permission.
This book, or parts thereof, may not be reproduced in any
form without permission in writing from the publisher,
PHILOMEL BOOKS,
a division of Penguin Putnam Books for Young Readers,
345 Hudson Street, New York, NY 10014.
Philomel Books, Reg. U.S. Pat. & Tm. Off.
Published simultaneously in Canada.
Manufactured in China by South China
Printing Co. Ltd.
Book design by Semadar Megged.
The text is set in 19-point Cheltenham BT.
The art was created using mixed media,
including gouache and computer techniques.

Library of Congress Cataloging-in-Publication Data
Fitzgerald, Ella.
A-tisket, a-tasket / by Ella Fitzgerald and Van Alexander;
illustrated by Ora Eitan.   p. cm.
Summary: A boy in New York City drops his green and yellow basket
and later sees a little girl carrying it around.
1. Children's songs—Texts. [1. Baskets—Songs and music.
2. Songs.] I. Alexander, Van. II. Eitan, Ora, 1940– ill. III. Title.
PZ8.3.F6356 At 2003   782.42164'0268—dc21
[E]   2002009020

ISBN 0-399-23206-0
1 2 3 4 5 6 7 8 9 10
First Impression

a- tisket a- tasket

by
ella fitzgerald
and
van alexander

illustrated by
ora eitan

Philomel Books · New York

CHASE BRANCH LIBRARY
17731 W. SEVEN MILE RD.
DETROIT, MI 48235

A-tisket, a-tasket, a green-and-yellow basket,
I wrote a letter to my mommy,

on the way I dropped it. I dropped it, I dropped it,
my little yellow basket.

A little girlie picked it up and took it to the market.

She was truckin' on down the avenue
without a single thing to do.

She went a-peck, peck, pecking all around
when she set it on the ground!

She took it, she took it, my little yellow basket,

and if she doesn't bring it back, I think that I shall die.

A-tisket, a-tasket, I lost my yellow basket,
and if that girlie don't return it, don't know what I will do.

Oh, dear, I wish that little girl I could see. *Have you seen her over there?*

Oh, gee, I wonder where my basket can be. *Have you seen my basket over here?*

Was it red? *No, no, no, no.*

Was it brown? *No, no, no, no.*

Was it blue? *No, no, no, no.* Just a little yellow basket.

A-tisket, a-tasket, I found my yellow basket.
I thought I lost it to that girlie,

but I found it after all.